The Pooped Troop

YOUNG YEARLING BOOKS YOU WILL ENJOY:

The Pee Wee Scout Books by Judy Delton

COOKIES AND CRUTCHES
CAMP GHOST-AWAY
LUCKY DOG DAYS
BLUE SKIES, FRENCH FRIES
GRUMPY PUMPKINS
PEANUT–BUTTER PILGRIMS
A PEE WEE CHRISTMAS
THAT MUSHY STUFF
SPRING SPROUTS
THE POOPED TROOP

YEARLING BOOKS/YOUNG YEARLINGS/YEARLING CLAS-
SICS are designed especially to entertain and
enlighten young people. Patricia Reilly Giff, consultant to this series, received the bachelor's
degree from Marymount College. She holds the
master's degree in history from St. John's University, and a Professional Diploma in Reading
from Hofstra University. She was a teacher and
reading consultant for many years, and is the
author of numerous books for young readers.

For a complete listing of all Yearling titles, write to
Dell Readers Service, P.O. Box 1045,
South Holland, IL 60473.

The Pooped Troop

JUDY DELTON

Illustrated by Alan Tiegreen

A YOUNG YEARLING BOOK

Published by
Dell Publishing
a division of
Bantam Doubleday Dell Publishing Group, Inc.
666 Fifth Avenue
New York, New York 10103

ISBN: 0-440-40184-4

Printed in the United States of America

June 1989

10 9 8 7 6 5 4

W

For George, who knew the Pee Wees before I did,

And with thanks to Lori Mack, exceptional editor

Contents

CHAPTER 1

No More Teachers

"**N**o more pencils," chanted Roger White. "No more books. No more teacher's dirty looks."

Roger made an airplane with his reading work sheet. He sailed it over Kevin Moe's head.

"And no more homework," added Kevin.

"I might go camping this summer," said Rachel Meyers. "With my dad."

"We're going to the lake," said Tracy Barnes. "Our whole family. To fish."

The second graders raced out of their room. They ran down the steps. Some of them went home. But the Pee Wee Scouts got on the big orange bus that was waiting. Waiting to take them to Mrs. Peters's house for a meeting. She was their troop leader.

Roger and Kevin got on the bus. They sat together.

Rachel and Tracy got on. And Molly Duff and Mary Beth Kelly.

"I feel bad that school is out," said Mary Beth. "I have to baby-sit for my little brother and sister all summer."

That didn't sound bad to Molly. She was an only child.

"I'll help with your little brother and sister," said Molly. "I'd love to baby-sit them."

"Okay," said Mary Beth. Molly was her best friend.

3

When they got to Mrs. Peters's house, the Scouts ran to her door. They couldn't wait for the meeting to start. They had their red kerchiefs on. And they all had good deeds to report.

But Mrs. Peters did not come to the door. She came riding down the street on a bicycle! Her baby, Nick, sat in the baby seat behind her.

"You were almost late!" shouted Sonny Betz. "Late for your own meeting!"

Mrs. Peters laughed and unlocked her door. After the Pee Wee Scouts sat down around the big table, she said, "I was getting in shape. For our Pee Wee Fitness Festival."

The Scouts looked surprised. They all began to talk at once. Mrs. Peters put up her hand. Then she clapped. The Scouts whispered. Mrs. Peters waited. Then she said, "How many of you like exercise?"

4

Some of the Scouts raised their hands. Some didn't.

"I like to skate," said Lisa Ronning.

"I like to play checkers," said Kenny Baker.

"Checkers aren't exercise," said Rachel.

"Oh, yeah?" said Kenny. "They play checkers in the Olympics!"

"Skiing is good exercise," said Tim Noon. "I watch them on TV. They ski down these big hills.

"Swoosh, swoosh, swoosh," Tim said. He moved his hips from side to side.

All the Scouts began to ski around the room.

"Zoom!" said Kenny.

"Skiers don't make any noise," said Mrs. Peters. "Snow is quiet."

"Swimming is good exercise too," said Rachel. "In the Olympics the swimmers get medals."

"Well," said Mrs Peters, "we are all going to exercise too. But instead of medals, we will get badges. And instead of skiing and skating, we will bike. And do aerobics. And we will do push-ups and play softball."

"I can't play softball," said Mary Beth to Molly.

Molly frowned.

"We'll all tune up our bodies," Mrs. Peters went on, "and we'll get in shape. And get a badge at the same time."

"I can't hit a softball," called Mary Beth.

"You'll learn," said Mrs. Peters. "We'll just take one sport at a time. And we'll all do just fine!"

Mary Beth looked doubtful.

"When we finish, we'll have a party," Mrs. Peters said. "We'll have good food, and we'll get our badges."

The Scouts cheered, "Yeah!"

"The first thing is bicycle riding. Does everyone have a bike?" asked Mrs. Peters.

Tim raised his hand. "I don't," he said. "Somebody stole it."

"I'll bet he never had one," whispered Tracy to Molly.

Molly felt sorry for Tim. His family was poor.

"Mrs. Peters! Mrs. Peters!" shouted Kevin. "He can borrow one of mine. I've got two."

"Thank you, Kevin," said Mrs. Peters. "Then we are all set. You can practice this week, now that school is out. And on Saturday morning we'll ride around the park. First, we'll divide up into two teams. Then we'll see how long it takes each team to get back to the statue of Ben Franklin."

"Yeah!" the Scouts cheered again.

Mrs. Peters talked about safe biking.

She talked about reading traffic signs. And watching for cars.

"My mom won't let me ride in the street," said Sonny.

"Baby," muttered Roger.

"It's not safe to ride on the sidewalk, Sonny. You could hit someone who is walking," said Mrs. Peters.

"Pow!" said Kevin. "Wham, bang!"

"What should I do?" Sonny asked. He looked like he might cry.

"I'll talk to your mother about it," said Mrs. Peters. "Don't worry."

Then she said to everyone, "Let's talk about the good deeds you did during the week."

Patty Baker waved her hand. She was Kenny's twin sister.

"I picked up my grandma's medicine at the drugstore," she said.

"Mrs. Peters?" called Tracy. "I opened

8

a childproof baby-aspirin bottle for my mom. She couldn't get the top off."

Molly wasn't sure if that was a good deed or not.

"I killed four flies with my speller,"

said Kenny. "They were bothering my dad."

"I found my little sister's shoes," said Tracy. "They were behind the piano. If I didn't find them, we couldn't have gone out for burgers. My dad said so."

"Molly, do you have a good deed this week?" asked Mrs. Peters.

"I did, but I forgot it," said Molly. "I forgot what it was."

"Mrs. Peters?" called Sonny. "I didn't wake my mom up last Sunday morning."

"Good for you, Sonny," said Mrs. Peters.

Mrs. Peters put cookies on the table. She poured some milk. When the Scouts finished eating, she said, "Now we'll sing our Pee Wee Scout song and say our Pee Wee Scout pledge."

The Pee Wees joined hands and sang. It felt good to Molly. She wished the song had more verses. She wanted to sing all day long.

"Have fun this week," said Mrs. Peters. "And be sure to be at the park at ten o'clock on Saturday morning."

CHAPTER 2

The Rockets and the Jets

When Molly got home, she put her old schoolbooks in her room. Then she went out to the garage and polished her bike. When her dad came home from work, he gave her an oil can. He showed her where to oil the wheels.

"Now you'll go fast," he said. "Fast and smooth."

The next morning Mary Beth came to Molly's door. "Let's practice for the race," she said. They walked toward school.

The school parking lot was empty. "This is a good spot," said Mary Beth.

Some of the other Pee Wee Scouts thought so too. They were already there.

"Look at my new bike," said Roger proudly.

The Scouts looked.

It was shiny.

It was fast.

It looked expensive.

"It's English," said Roger. "Those guys in England win races on these things." He patted the leather seat. "It's got ten speeds, and hand brakes too."

Roger got on.

The Scouts watched him ride his bike back and forth across the lot.

"I hope he's on our team," whispered Mary Beth to Molly.

"I wonder if we get to pick whose team we want to be on," said Molly.

"Probably not," said Mary Beth. "But if we do, I'll pick Roger's."

Tim came down the street on a wobbly bike. It was Kevin's old one. He weaved from side to side. "This thing is lopsided," he said. "It's all rusty too."

Back and forth. Back and forth, the Scouts pedaled. Molly could ride fast. She pretended she was chasing a racehorse. She pedaled faster and faster.

"The park is real small," said Roger. "My team can get around there in no time. We'll win easy."

Every day the Scouts pedaled around the parking lot. They got better and better. Most of them.

But Tim still seemed wobbly.

"What if he's on our team instead of Roger?" said Mary Beth.

"We'll lose," said Molly glumly.

On Saturday morning Molly was the first one at the park.

Then Mrs. Peters came. They sat on a bench in the shade and waited for the others.

Tracy came next with her little sister in the baby seat behind her. "I have to baby-sit her," she said.

"She can sit here and watch with me," said Mrs. Peters.

Tim came wobbling down the street slowly. Then came Rachel on her ten-speed. She had a white wicker basket on her handlebars.

Rachel could go fast. She was a good biker. Molly hoped she would be on her team.

Soon everyone was at the park but Sonny.

"While we are waiting for Sonny,"

said Mrs. Peters, "we will draw for teams."

She shook a paper bag.

"There are eleven slips of paper in here. Some say Jets and some say Rockets," she said.

Mrs. Peters shook the bag again.

"Now each of you draw one," she said.

Molly was the first to draw. "Jets," she said.

Mary Beth drew next. "I'm on your team!" she cried.

Then Rachel drew Rockets.

"Darn!" said Molly. "We needed her on our team."

Roger drew Rockets too. Molly groaned.

Patty and Kenny drew Jets. Tim drew Jets.

"We're doomed," Molly muttered.

Soon all the slips were drawn but one.

17

"This last one is Sonny's," said Mrs. Peters. She took the slip out and read it.

"Sonny is on the Jets," she said.

"Is Sonny a good biker?" whispered Lisa to Molly.

"I don't know," said Molly. "I never saw him ride a bike."

The Scouts looked down the street for Sonny. They couldn't start without him.

Soon a car drove up. It stopped. It was Sonny's mother. With Sonny.

Mrs. Betz jumped out and opened the trunk of the car. She took out a very small bike and set it on the sidewalk. Then she waved and said, "I'm off to the dentist."

She drove away.

The Scouts stared at Sonny's bike.

"What an iddy-biddy bike!" Rachel laughed.

"Ho, ho, it's a girl's bike!" shouted Roger.

It didn't bother Molly that the bike was small.

Or that it was a girl's bike.

Or that it had a basket on the front with plastic flowers on it.

What bothered Molly was that the bike stood up by itself on the sidewalk.

"Training wheels!" shouted Molly. "Why are there training wheels on your bike?"

"I'm just learning to balance," said Sonny.

Now all of the Jets groaned. Who could win a race with training wheels?

"How come you didn't learn to ride a two-wheeler in first grade?" demanded Kevin.

"I could ride one when I was five," boasted Tim.

"I could ride one when I was three," said Roger.

"My mom says I am too young to ride a two-wheeler," said Sonny.

"What *can* you ride, a trike?" Lisa laughed.

"Or a kiddy car!" shrieked Rachel.

Mrs. Peters held up her hand. "Sonny will do the best he can," she said. "Now all the Rockets line up over here on this side of the park." Mrs. Peters pointed.

"And the Jets will go on the other side. It isn't important to ride fast. Just steadily and safely. Keep big spaces between you."

The Scouts scrambled to get in their places.

"There's no way we can win," said Molly.

"We're licked," said Patty.

Sonny tried to get on his bike. It fell over on top of him.

Mrs. Peters helped him up. "Are you sure you can ride it?" she asked.

Sonny nodded.

Tim was wobbling even before they began.

"Rat's knees!" said Molly.

Mrs. Peters said, "Get on your mark, get set, go!"

The park was very small. Molly was around it in no time. So were Mary Beth and Lisa and Rachel. Tim wobbled from one side to the other. Behind him Sonny was moving very very slowly.

Roger and Rachel were in the lead for the Rockets.

"Yeah, Rockets!" the rest of their team shouted.

"Yeah, Jets!" shouted Molly and Mary Beth.

All of a sudden Roger slowed down to
a stop. The Rockets stopped shouting.

Something was the matter.

"My pants are caught in the chain!"
shouted Roger. He tugged and tugged to
try to get them out.

Mrs. Peters ran over to help. Mean-
while, Sonny and Tim pedaled slowly.

Now all the Rockets were finished,
except Roger.

And all the Jets were finished, but Sonny.

"Come on, Roger," shouted the Rockets.

But Roger couldn't move.

"Come on, Sonny!" shouted the Jets.

Roger pulled on his pants leg.

Rachel pulled on it.

They tried to push Roger. They tried to make him go forward. But his bike wouldn't budge!

Sonny kept moving.

Pedal, pedal, pedal.

Closer and closer.

Finally he crossed over the finish line.

"We won!" cried Molly. The Jets jumped up and down and hugged one another.

They patted Sonny on the back.

"Sonny won for us! Sonny won for us!" shouted Mary Beth.

"Sonny could have crawled around the

park and still won," said Kevin. "Roger still can't move!"

Kevin was right.

Roger's fancy bike was broken.

CHAPTER 3

Underwear Trouble

"**W**e will give the badges out when our Fitness Festival is over," said Mrs. Peters. It was the next Tuesday. The Pee Wees were having a Scout meeting at Mrs. Peters's house.

"I wonder if Roger will get a badge," whispered Molly. "He lost that race for the Rockets."

Roger didn't look happy. Mrs. Peters had had to cut his pants to get them out of the chain. And his dad hadn't fixed his bike yet.

"In the Fitness Festival," said Mrs. Peters, "a Scout only competes with himself or herself. We do our best to make our bodies strong. Now I want to tell you about our next sport," she said. "There will be three more sports. Push-ups, aerobic dancing, and hitting a softball."

"I can't hit a softball," whined Mary Beth.

"It's simple," said Roger.

"You said the bike race was simple too," Tracy reminded him.

"I can hit a ball blindfolded," said Kevin. "Plus all that other stuff."

"I can too," said Rachel.

Molly wasn't sure about aerobic dancing.

Mrs. Peters seemed to read Molly's mind. "Mrs. Betz is going to take you to her health club and teach you how to do aerobic dance," she said. "It's good exercise. And it helps you breathe right."

"I can breathe all right," said Tim. He breathed in and out loudly.

Soon all the Scouts were breathing loudly.

In and out.

In and out.

"The same with softball," said Mrs. Peters. "There will be lots of time to practice. To get your Fitness badge all you have to do is hit the ball."

"How many times?" asked Tim.

"Once is enough," said Mrs. Peters.

Mary Beth looked worried. "I can't do it," she said. "I can't hit a ball with a bat."

"I'll show you how to play softball," said Molly.

"I know *how*," said Mary Beth. "I just can't hit the ball."

"We'll think of something," said Molly. "Don't worry."

But Mary Beth did worry. She looked worried during the whole meeting.

"Today we are going to do push-ups," Mrs. Peters was saying. "We'll work outside. It's nice and sunny. I put some old blankets out on the grass."

The Scouts followed Mrs. Peters outside. They stood in a circle. She showed them how to do a push-up.

"One two, one two, one two," she said, as she lifted her body on her hands. Her feet stuck out behind her. "Remember, keep your knees up. Off the ground."

Mrs. Peters took a deep breath. "To get the badge," she went on, "you must do five push-ups."

"No problem," said Roger, dropping down to the ground.

The Scouts watched. Roger did perfect push-ups. Knees off the ground.

"One!" the Scouts counted. "Two! Three! Four! Five!"

Roger was not even out of breath. He jumped to his feet.

"It looks like Roger is in pretty good shape," said Mrs. Peters. "Now let's see the rest of you try it!"

Sonny tried it. Splat. He fell flat on his stomach.

"Now me," said Tim. He stretched his neck forward like a turtle.

Patty tried it.

"Not on your elbows!" called Mrs. Peters.

It was Molly's turn. She couldn't lift her body off the ground!

Not her knees.

Not her stomach.

Not her chest.

Not her elbows.

Something kept her down. Something tight.

"One two," said Mrs. Peters. "One two, and up!"

But Molly did not go up. She was still flat on the ground.

It's my underwear, she said to herself. My underwear is too tight.

She would have to take it off. She thought how good it would feel to just have on her loose shorts. Loose and roomy. She could do perfect push-ups then.

But what would her mother say? Or Mrs. Peters? No one went outside without underwear. What if she had to go to the hospital? What if she broke her leg?

Her mother had told Molly that under-wear always had to be neat and clean. But Molly's was too tight!

Rachel did five perfect push-ups in a row. So did Tracy. Even Sonny did two.

Would Molly be the only one without a Fitness badge?

CHAPTER 4

An Accident

If she had a scissors, she could cut her underwear. So she could breathe better. She wondered if Mrs. Peters had a scissors.

If she ran home to change, the Scout meeting would be over. She would miss her chance to do five push-ups. It would be too late.

Lisa was watching her. "What's the matter?" she asked.

"My underwear's too tight," whispered Molly. "I can't bend."

"Stretch it," said Lisa. "Pull it real hard. It will get looser. That's what I do."

"Really?" said Molly. She waited till no one was looking. Then she gave a big tug on her underwear. Nothing happened. She tugged again. Hard. She pulled it as far as it would go.

All of a sudden the elastic broke. Snap!

"What was that?" said Roger.

Everyone looked around.

Molly looked around.

"Who else can do push-ups?" asked Mrs. Peters. "Last call for today."

"Me!" Molly got down on the ground. It was easy now. She put her hands down and her elbows up. One two. Nothing happened. She tried again. Push. She lifted her chest up. Push. She got her stomach up.

"Lift those knees!" said Mrs. Peters.

Molly did. She held herself up on her hands and toes.

Mrs. Peters clapped. "You did it!" she said. "Now just practice and you can do it five times!"

Molly tried again. Then a third time. Four! Five!

Everyone cheered, "Yeah!"

"And that's all for today," said Mrs. Peters.

Molly was exhausted.

"Everyone stand in a circle, please. Let's sing our song and say our pledge and call it a day," said Mrs. Peters.

"How do you call it a day?" asked Tim.

"It is a day," said Sonny.

"It's just an expression, dummy," said Rachel.

The Scouts joined hands and sang their Pee Wee Scout song. Then they said the Pee Wee Scout pledge.

During the song Roger was laughing. So was Sonny. Before long everyone was laughing.

Molly didn't know why everyone was laughing, but she began to laugh too.

Then Roger pointed at her. He kept laughing.

Patty whispered in Molly's ear, "Your underwear is hanging out."

Molly looked down. Oh, no. Underwear trouble! She still had it. She ran into the house and into the bathroom.

She took her saggy underwear off. She crumpled it up and put it into Mrs. Peters's wastebasket. She buried it deep. On the very bottom.

When she came out, Mrs. Peters was saying, "Anyone can have an accident, boys and girls. It is not polite to laugh at accidents."

Molly didn't join the circle of Scouts.

She slipped out of the yard and ran all the way home.

When Molly got home, she went into her room and closed the door. She cried a little bit about her saggy underwear.

Then she went into the kitchen. The phone rang. It was Mary Beth.

"You left so fast, you didn't hear what Mrs. Peters said. On Saturday we have to meet at the health spa. Mrs. Betz is going to show us how to do aerobic dancing."

Molly didn't know what *aerobic* meant.

"You can ride with me," Mary Beth said. "My dad is driving me. At nine o'clock."

"Thanks," said Molly. She hung up.

"We have aerobic dancing next Saturday," Molly told her mother. She didn't tell her mother about the underwear trouble.

"I'll be out of town visiting Grandma this weekend," said Mrs. Duff. "But Dad will be here. You better eat foods with lots of vitamins and get in shape. That is hard work."

Molly wondered how dancing could be hard work. But, anyway, she was used to hard work.

Push-ups were hard work.

School was hard work.

Biking was hard work.

On Saturday, Molly wondered what to wear for aerobic dance. If it was hard work, she should wear overalls. But if it was dancing, she should wear a good dress. She decided on the dress. Dancers on TV wore little skirts. Rachel would probably wear a fancy dance outfit.

When Molly got into Mary Beth's car, she wished she had worn pants. Mary Beth had on jeans.

CHAPTER 5

Shake Your Shape

When Molly and Mary Beth walked into the spa, all the other Scouts were there. In swimsuits! And sneakers. Mary Beth took off her jeans. She had a swimsuit on too!

"Why didn't you tell me we were supposed to wear swimsuits?" whispered Molly crossly.

"I forgot," said Mary Beth.

Mary Beth was making Molly mad. She forgot to tell her important things. And she was always whining about softball. Some best friend.

Mrs. Betz had on a leotard. It was long and black and shiny. It was skintight. She had a sweatband around her forehead. Some of the Scouts had sweatbands on too.

Sonny had on a leotard just like his mother's. Only it was red. The Scouts laughed at him.

"He looks like a sausage," said Roger.

"Or a red banana," Kevin snickered.

"That's what all dancers wear," said Rachel. She looked at Molly. "How come you've got a dress on?"

"I didn't know about wearing swimsuits," said Molly.

"That's because you left the meeting early," said Rachel.

Everyone stood around on the mats, getting ready.

Molly tried to stretch in her blue dotted-swiss dress. She was the only one with shoes on. She wore patent-leather shoes with black bows.

"You better take your shoes off, Molly," called Mrs. Betz. "It isn't good for the gym floor. Besides, you can't stretch your toes with those shoes on."

"On your way to a wedding?"said Roger. "Let's see your underwear!" He bent over in laughter. "Ho, ho!"

Molly's face was red. She wished she had never heard of a Fitness Festival.

"Where is Mrs. Peters?" asked Molly.

Mrs. Betz said, "Mrs. Peters is out of town. She'll be back for the next meeting."

"My mom is out of town too," Molly whispered to Lisa.

"I'm your leader today," Mrs. Betz went on. "This is Miss Tucker. She is the aerobics teacher here at the spa."

Miss Tucker smiled. She had a leotard on too. And a blond ponytail. She looked healthy.

"Sonny and I work out with Miss Tucker every weekend," Mrs. Betz said.

The Scouts giggled. Sonny worked out.

Mrs. Betz had a little rip in the seam of her leotard.

"Her suit might pop!" whispered Mary Beth to Molly. "It's so tight. Look."

"I hope it doesn't," said Molly.

But when Mrs. Betz bent over, the hole got bigger. When she stood up, it got smaller.

Molly wondered if she should tell her. But she didn't want to disturb the class.

Miss Tucker told the Scouts about healthy aerobic dancing. "*Aerobic* means air," she said. "It's a dance that helps you breathe well."

44

She told them how to stretch and breathe in. Stretch and breathe out.

"Feel your lungs expand!" shouted Mrs. Betz.

She breathed in and out.

In and out.

So did the Scouts.

Miss Tucker put some music on. She showed the Scouts how to stretch and bend to the music. She showed them how to jog in place.

She walked up and down the row of Scouts. Clapping. Watching to make sure they did it right.

"Knees high!" she called, lifting up Tracy's leg. "Lift those knees! Swing those arms!

"Now," Miss Tucker shouted, "step and skip! Step and skip!"

"It's hard to do it so fast!" cried Molly. She tried to keep up. Step and skip.

Tim and Tracy were still jogging in place.

Step and skip.

"Reach high," called Miss Tucker. "Reach up high and touch the sky!" she called. The music got louder and faster.

The Pee Wees reached high. Except Tim. He was still jogging in place.

"Stretch and bend!" sang Miss Tucker. "Stretch and bend."

The Scouts were tired.

Patty's face was red.

Kenny was panting and puffing.

Mrs. Betz slapped him on the back. "Shake your shape!" she shouted. "Tune up that body!"

Soon the Scouts were worn out. When Miss Tucker said, "Rest time," they all collapsed on the mats.

No one talked.

No one moved.

The Scouts lay on the mats, exhausted.

Mrs. Betz and Miss Tucker kept dancing.

Sonny went out and came back with carrot juice. Little cans for everyone. He had to make three trips.

"I want some soda pop," moaned Roger.

"Soda makes you thirsty," said Mrs.

Betz. "It's full of sugar and chemicals. This will build those bodies."

Molly didn't want to build her body. Neither did Mary Beth. They just wanted to get their badges.

As soon as the Scouts finished their carrot juice, Miss Tucker said, "Here we go!" and turned the music on again. The Scouts groaned.

Sonny stood up as straight as a stick. He kicked his legs like a wooden soldier.

"One, two, three, kick!" called Miss Tucker. "Shoulders back! Stomach in!"

Sonny's back was straight.

His stomach was in.

"He's good," said Lisa.

"No wonder," said Mary Beth. "He's had lots of practice."

Miss Tucker showed the Scouts how to roll their heads.

"Tune up those muscles!" called Mrs. Betz. "You can do it!"

"My head is going to roll off!" cried Molly.

"When is this going to be over?" groaned Lisa.

In the big mirror Molly could see the long row of Pee Wee Scouts. Tired, tired Scouts. It was a lot of work for a badge. More work than the Pee Wees had ever done.

"I'm pooped," said Molly.

"This whole troop is pooped!" shouted Rachel.

At last Miss Tucker said, "We'll stop for today." She blew her whistle. "Now we'll head for the showers."

Molly didn't want a shower. She wanted to go home. She just wanted to take off her itchy dress.

"Next week is softball," whined Mary Beth as they walked to the showers. "How am I going to hit that ball?"

Molly was tired of Mary Beth whining. Maybe she was tired of Mary Beth!

Molly was hot.

She was tired.

She itched and ached.

Maybe, she thought, I need a new best friend.

CHAPTER 6
Molly's Ex-Best Friend

The next morning Molly's phone rang. It was Lisa.

"Let's go to the park and play ball," Lisa said. "I'll pitch and you can hit the ball. Then we can switch and you can pitch to me."

"Okay," said Molly. She needed practice if she was going to get a badge. Mary Beth wasn't the only one who had trouble hitting a ball.

What about Mary Beth? thought Molly

as she pulled on her shorts. I should call her and ask her to come along.

But she didn't. Molly ran out the door instead.

She grabbed a ball and bat from the garage. She tried to forget about Mary Beth's problem.

Lisa was waiting on a bench. She looked like a good best friend. A better best friend than Mary Beth. Lisa wasn't whining. She was smiling.

"Hi," Lisa called. She was swinging her bat. "I'll pitch to you first."

Molly stood like the baseball players she had seen on TV. Lisa threw the ball. Right to Molly.

Molly swung her bat. Swish! The ball sailed past Molly's shoulder.

"I missed it!" cried Molly.

"Hold the bat lower," said Lisa. She

ran over and showed Molly how to hold it. "Now I'll pitch again."

Lisa swung her arm around and around. Then she let go of the ball.

Swish! Molly's bat went right through the empty air. The ball flew past her.

After another try Lisa yelled, "You're out! It's my turn to bat."

"I'm as bad as Mary Beth," cried Molly.

"You'll catch on," said Lisa. "You just need practice."

They switched places. Molly pitched the ball to Lisa. CRACK! Lisa hit the ball. It sailed through the park.

"Wow!" shouted Molly. She turned and chased the ball. When she finally got it, she jogged back to her spot.

"That would be a home run," said Lisa, "if we were playing a real game."

"I know it," said Molly.

Roger and Kevin rode up on their bikes. Roger's dad had fixed his bike.

Kevin had a ball and bat with him. "I'm up first!" he shouted. He jumped off his bike and leaned it against a tree. "Watch this," he called to the girls.

The girls sat on a bench to rest. And to watch.

Roger pitched a ball to Kevin.

SMACK! Kevin hit the ball. Just like Lisa.

"Look at that thing go!" yelled Roger.

"My dad says I'll be a pro when I grow up!" said Kevin. He jumped around.

"Show-off," muttered Molly.

"It's my turn," said Roger.

Kevin pitched the ball fast. Very fast.

Roger hit it high into the air. But not as far as Kevin.

"Let's try again," said Lisa. "I'll pitch you some easy ones."

Molly held her bat up. She kept her eye on the ball.

Lisa threw the ball. It hit the bat and Molly hadn't even swung it! It bounced on the ground in front of her.

"It's easy!" said Molly. "Let's do it again."

This time Molly swung the bat. She hit the ball.

"All right!" said Lisa.

Just then the Scouts heard a loud yell.

"Hey! How come you went to play ball without me?"

It was Mary Beth.

Oh, no, thought Molly.

"Come on," called Lisa. "We can all take turns."

Mary Beth pouted, but she took the bat. Lisa pitched.

But Mary Beth didn't even try to hit the ball. She just stood and cried.

Molly stamped her foot. "Rat's knees!"
she said. "You have to try!"

"My mom says I'm not athletic," Mary
Beth whimpered. "No one in our family
is athletic."

"You pitch," said Lisa. "Maybe that's easier."

"But I won't get a badge if I don't hit the ball," sobbed Mary Beth.

Molly knew how she felt. It would be awful to be the only one without the Fitness badge.

The girls sat down to rest. Roger hit ball after ball. So did Kevin. Smack, swish, crack!

"Girls can't play baseball," shrieked Roger. He swung the bat around and around.

"We can too!" shouted Molly.

"Let's go practice in my backyard," said Lisa.

The girls gathered their things and left the boys behind.

When they got to Lisa's, her mother brought out ice-cream cones. And lemonade. The girls sat on the back steps.

"Let's call it a day," said Molly. "I'm tired."

Lisa giggled. "You sound like Mrs. Peters," she said.

Mary Beth was not giggling. She wasn't even smiling. Soon it would be Tuesday. The day they had to hit the ball for Mrs. Peters.

CHAPTER 7

Batter Up!

On Tuesday the Pee Wee Scouts met in the park. They carried balls and bats.

Sonny had a catcher's mitt. He was wearing a face mask too.

"My mom says softballs aren't very soft," he said.

"Line up!" called Mrs. Peters.

The Scouts got in a row. Kevin was begging Mrs. Peters to let him pitch.

"No," she said. "We have to have a pitcher who is not a Scout."

Just then Mr. Peters drove up in the van. He waved to the Scouts.

"Here is the pitcher now!" said Mrs. Peters.

"Batter up!" called Mr. Peters as he jumped out of the van and got ready to pitch the ball.

First he pitched to Patty. "You get three tries," said Mr. Peters. "If you don't hit the ball after three pitches, you can go to the end of the line and try again."

Patty hit the ball on her second try. Not far, but she hit it.

Kevin was at the end of the line. "Girls are sissies," he said. "They can't hit the ball far."

Mr. Peters pitched the ball to Kenny. He hit the third pitch.

"Just in time," Tracy snickered.

Tim hit the ball the first time.

"Yeah, Tim!" Kevin whistled through his teeth.

Sonny was up next. He waved the bat in the air and dropped it. "It's too heavy!" he cried.

Mrs. Peters handed him a lighter bat.

Finally Sonny hit the ball. He hit the third pitch.

Mary Beth was next. Molly gave her a push. But instead of going up to bat, Mary Beth ran around to the end of the line.

Now Rachel was up to bat. She gave the ball a good whack. It went up and over the swing set.

"Good for you!" shouted Mrs. Peters.

Kevin was next.

"Now watch the champ!" shouted Roger. "Yeah, Kevin!"

Kevin smiled. He looked sure of himself. He pulled his cap down. He even spit on the ground.

Whiz! Mr. Peters threw a fast pitch. It flew past Kevin's bat. The Scouts were quiet. Kevin had missed his first ball.

Mr. Peters threw the next ball. Kevin swung. Whoosh! The bat went through the air.

Kevin's face got red. He spit again.

Mr. Peters pitched.

Kevin missed.

"Strike three, you're out!" shouted Mary Beth. "You're out, you're out, you're out!" She jumped up and down.

The girls began to clap.

The boys booed.

"Ha, ha, who's a sissy now!" called Tracy.

Kevin went to the end of the line. Lisa took her turn and hit the first pitch.

At last Mary Beth was up at bat. She looked like she was going to cry. But she took the bat and marched up to the plate. She meant business.

Mr. Peters pitched the ball.

SMACK! Mary Beth hit it. It flew out over the park fence. Farther than anyone had hit! She dropped the bat and jumped up and down.

"Good work!" said Mrs. Peters.

The Scouts cheered.

Then Molly took her turn. She hit the ball high into the air. It went high and far. But it went behind them. The wrong way.

The Scouts heard a thud. After the thud came a tinkling sound. Like something breaking. Was it glass?

"Oh, no," said Mrs. Peters. "I don't like the sound of that."

"Uh, oh," said Lisa.

The Scouts followed Mr. and Mrs. Peters. They ran past a few oak trees. Soon they found Molly's ball. On top of some broken glass.

"A garage window," said Tim. "Molly broke a window!"

"Molly's gonna get it, Molly's gonna get it!" sang Roger.

"It wasn't your fault," said Mary Beth.

"It is just one pane," said Mr. Peters. "It must have broken the glass when it

bounced off the pane. We'll fix that this afternoon."

Mrs. Peters knocked on the door of the house and explained everything to the man who answered the door.

"I thought I heard a noise out in the garage," he said.

"We'll fix it today," said Mr. Peters.

"That must have been some home run," said the man, laughing.

"A home run the wrong way," Tim snickered.

"Don't worry about it," Mrs. Peters said to Molly. "You didn't even know the garage was there."

"But what will my mom and dad say?" asked Molly. She had tears in her eyes.

"I'll talk to your mom and dad," said Mr. Peters cheerfully. "Don't worry."

Mary Beth put her arm around Molly.

It felt good to have a friend to lean on. It made Molly feel a little better.

"At least you hit the ball," said Mary Beth.

She was right. Molly had hit the ball. And Mary Beth had gotten a hit too. The Fitness Festival wasn't so bad after all.

The Scouts went back to the field to finish up. Kevin was the only one who still needed a hit.

"Batter up!" called Mr. Peters. "Let's see Kevin hit that ball now. Let's see him earn that badge."

Everyone began to cheer for Kevin. Even the girls.

"Yeah, Moe! Yeah, Moe! Come on, Kevin, go go go!" yelled Roger.

Mr. Peters threw the ball. It hit Kevin's bat and bounced off. Before anyone could argue, Mrs. Peters shouted, "A hit! A hit! Good for you, Kevin!"

The Pee Wees cheered.

Kevin threw down the bat and walked away. He didn't brag. He didn't yell. He was embarrassed.

"That wasn't even a real hit," said Rachel.

"I can't be perfect all the time," muttered Kevin.

"Well!" said Mrs. Peters brightly. "Our Fitness Festival is over. Next Tuesday we'll celebrate at my house. Let's wear all our badges this time."

The Scouts picked up their bats and balls and started home. They walked together.

"I'm glad the Fitness Festival is over," said Mary Beth.

"Me too," said Molly. "Fitness is a lot of work."

"I'm never going to play softball again," said Rachel.

"Or do another push-up," said Tracy.

"Or do aerobic dancing," said Tim.

"I am," said Sonny. "I have to go with my mom on Saturday."

"Too bad for you," said Molly.

"It's okay," said Sonny. "It keeps me in good shape."

CHAPTER 8

Pee Wees Forever

The Pee Wees rested all week. They didn't ride bikes. They didn't do push-ups. They didn't dance. Except Sonny. And they didn't think of playing softball. Not even once.

"Next Tuesday we get our badges," said Lisa on Sunday afternoon. The girls were sitting on Molly's steps.

"I can't wait," said Mary Beth. "My blouse is going to be full of badges."

"We'll have to put badges on our shorts pretty soon," said Lisa.

"Or down our arms!" said Mary Beth.

"On top of our heads!" shouted Molly.

"What are you going to bring to the party?" asked Mary Beth.

"Fruit salad," said Molly. "Lisa and I are going to make it together."

Mary Beth looked hurt.

"I thought we could make something together, just you and me," whispered Mary Beth to Molly. "Like when we made cookies for the cookie badge."

Mary Beth is jealous, thought Molly.

"I thought we were best friends," Mary Beth said into Molly's ear. "Aren't we?"

Molly liked Mary Beth. She missed doing things with her alone like they used to. Mary Beth knew all about Molly's feelings. And she understood her problems.

"Well, aren't we?" Mary Beth demanded.

"Of course," said Molly. "How about

having a picnic next Wednesday, just the two of us?"

Mary Beth smiled.

"But we can all make fruit salad together on Tuesday," said Molly. "All three of us."

"We can make it at my house," said Lisa.

"I'll bring some apples," said Mary Beth.

"I'll bring whatever my mom has in the refrigerator," said Molly.

When the girls left, Mary Beth wasn't pouting. She was in a good mood again. Molly was glad.

Soon Tuesday came. It was the day of the Pee Wee Scout meeting. The day of the party!

At noon Molly and Mary Beth went to Lisa's house to make the salad.

"I've got peaches," said Molly. "And a melon."

"I brought apples and oranges," said Mary Beth.

"We've got cherries," said Lisa. "And bananas."

Lisa got out a big bowl. It wasn't big enough. When the girls tried to put the fruit in it, only four apples fit.

Lisa looked in the cupboard. The only thing that was big enough was a roaster pan.

"My mom cooks turkey in this," she said.

"It's just right," said Mary Beth. She piled all the fruit in it. It came all the way to the top.

"Something is the matter," said Molly, frowning.

"It doesn't look like fruit salad," said Mary Beth.

"It's so big," said Molly. "Maybe we have to cut it up."

"My mom said we aren't allowed to use knives," said Lisa. "She said we might cut ourselves if we used knives."

"Where is she?" asked Molly.

"Just next door," said Lisa. "She'll be back any minute."

The girls looked at the fruit.

"I know!" cried Molly. "It needs to be peeled! We can peel the bananas and oranges without a knife."

The girls peeled the bananas and oranges. But the melon peel wouldn't budge.

"That's okay," said Lisa. "Fruit salad is just fruit mixed up. That's what this is."

"The melon looks too big," said Molly.

"We'll put it on the bottom," said Mary Beth.

"Now it looks good," said Molly. "Yum."

"Good and healthy," said Lisa.

"It's time for the meeting!" said Mary Beth.

The girls started for Mrs. Peters's house. All three of them carried the roaster pan full of fruit salad. It was so heavy. On the way they met the other Scouts.

Everyone was carrying food.

Sonny had bran muffins.

Kenny and Patty had oatmeal cookies.

"Hey!" yelled Roger. "Is that a turkey?" He pointed to the roaster pan. "Hey, guys, it's Thanksgiving!"

"It's fruit salad," said Molly.

Roger looked into the pan.

"Salad!" he shrieked. "It looks like a grocery store!"

"Mind your own business," muttered Lisa.

When the Scouts got to Mrs. Peters's house, they were all surprised. In the backyard were rows of chairs. And all their parents!

"We came to celebrate the Fitness Festival too," said Mrs. Duff. "And eat some healthful food."

The girls set the roaster pan on the table with the other food.

"That looks very healthful," said Mrs. Baker, looking into the pan.

"What a lovely fruit salad," exclaimed Mrs. Peters.

"See," said Lisa to Roger. "Mrs. Peters knew what it was."

"I'll just break up these bananas," said Mrs. Peters with a little chuckle. "And I'll trim the melon a bit so we can all get some."

Before they knew it Mrs. Peters had made the fruit look more like salad.

"Look at all this good stuff!" said Molly.

The table was loaded down with good food.

Cookies.

Juice.

Vegetables and dip.

All good fitness food.

"Look!" said Tracy, pointing. "Here comes a bunch of other kids. What are they doing here?"

When they got closer, the Scouts could see they had blue kerchiefs around their necks. Just like their own red ones!

"Troop 15," said Roger. "Those are the guys we creamed in the football game!"

The blue Pee Wees.

Mrs. Peters blew her whistle.

"Welcome to our Fitness Festival," she said. "Before we eat, we'll play some games. And after we eat, we'll give out badges. Have fun!" she added.

The two Pee Wee Scout troops had fun together.

They played Duck Duck Goose. Then they played Red Rover with the moms and dads.

When everyone was worn out from playing games, it was time to eat.

"I'm not eating that grocery store!" said Roger, pointing to the roaster pan.

But everyone else did. Before long the

fruit salad was all gone. The pan was empty.

Soon all of the food was gone.

"I ate about two hundred cherries," said Molly, spitting out the last pit.

"What a good dinner," said Roger's father, patting his stomach. "That fruit salad really hit the spot."

Molly poked Roger in the ribs.

"Now," said Mrs. Peters, "it's time for the Fitness badges."

One at a time Mrs. Peters called out each Scout's name. Everyone clapped as the Scouts went up to get their badges.

"This one is my favorite badge," Molly whispered to Mary Beth.

It said FITNESS BADGE on it in yellow letters. In the middle was a Pee Wee Scout doing some push-ups. The Scout had on a red swimsuit. And hair the same color as Molly's.

Molly pinned the new badge on her shorts. Her whole blouse was already covered with badges.

She felt proud. Some of the things had been hard work. But the Pee Wee Scouts did them anyway.

"Aren't we going to talk about good deeds?" whispered Mary Beth to Molly. "I've got a good deed to tell."

"Save it for next time," said Molly. "At a regular meeting. This is a party."

"I want to tell Mrs. Peters about how you and Lisa helped me hit the ball."

"Really?" said Molly.

That was nice of Mary Beth, thought Molly. She was glad Mary Beth was still her best friend.

Soon the sun began to set over Mrs. Peters's garage. Baby Nick fell asleep in his stroller. The grown-ups sat and talked under the birch trees. And the Pee Wees stretched out on the grass to rest.

Molly and Mary Beth looked for four-leaf clovers.

Rachel and Lisa looked for the first star of the evening.

And Sonny and Roger showed the other Scouts all their badges.

Mrs. Peters stood up. "It's time for our Fitness Festival to come to an end," she said.

The Pee Wee Scouts groaned. No one wanted to leave.

"But first," Mrs. Peters went on, "we will make a big, big circle. We'll say our Pee Wee Scout pledge and sing our Pee Wee Scout song."

Both troops of Scouts stood up. The grown-ups did too. They all held hands in a big circle.

The circle went all the way around Mrs. Peters's big yard. Around the tables and chairs. Around the trees. Lucky and Tiny barked and chased each other in the middle.

Lisa stood on one side of Molly. Molly held her hand. Mary Beth was on the other side of Molly. Molly held her hand too.

When they said the pledge, Molly gave Mary Beth's hand a squeeze. It was fun to be a Scout. And it was fun to have a best friend.

Then they sang the Pee Wee Scout song. The singing was loud and strong.

It gave Molly goose bumps on her arms. It was a good feeling. She wanted to hug everyone. Even Roger!

As the Scouts and parents started to leave, Mrs. Peters waved good-bye. "Keep fit!" she called.

The Pee Wee Scouts and their parents waved back as they started for home.

"Pee Wees forever!" shouted Roger, and everyone laughed.

Pee Wee Scout Song

(to the tune of
"Old MacDonald Had a Farm")

Scouts are helpers, Scouts have fun,
Pee Wee, Pee Wee Scouts!
We sing and play when work is done,
Pee Wee, Pee Wee Scouts!

With a good deed here,
And an errand there,
Here a hand, there a hand,
Everywhere a good hand.

Scouts are helpers, Scouts have fun,
Pee Wee, Pee Wee Scouts!

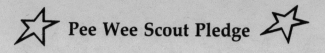 **Pee Wee Scout Pledge**

We love our country
And our home,
Our school and neighbors too.

As Pee Wee Scouts
We pledge our best
In everything we do.